Three Diaries

Three Diaries

By DC Fidler

DCFidler Publishing
2018

Published by DCFidler Publishing
1117 University Avenue, #505
Morgantown, WV 26505
DCFidlerpublishing@gmail.com

Printed in the United States of America
by Lulu Press, Inc.

This play is entirely a work of fiction.
Any resemblance to actual persons, living or dead,
is entirely coincidental.

ISBN: 978-0-9989729-7-8
Library of Congress Control Number: 2018905746

Three Diaries premiered at M.T. Pockets Theatre in Morgantown, West Virginia on October 25, 2007.

Original Cast

Janet Kenny	Breana Linder
Barry Grotsky	Michael Workman
Lawrence J. Greene	Matthew Tolliver

Additional Cast for Original Production

Franklin Kenny	Walter Hurd
Frank Martin	Scott Graham / Clif Wilson
Etta Greene	Angela Lacey-McCracken
Mrs. Holmes	Carmen Fullmer
Sue Lynn Martin	Angie McCombs / Glynis Board
Senator Holmes	Gary Insch
Charles Portego	Eddie Freedom
John Kenny	Reese Cochran
James Kenny	Jordan Munsey
Angela Andrade	Celcila Pucci
Darlene Yates	Meg Hersman
Taylor Manning	Meg Hersman
George Garringer	Christopher Odgen

Staff

Director	Glynis Board
Lighting Design	Kelly McGill
Costume Design	Michaela Sulka
Stage Manager	Nora Perone
Producers	Vickie Trickett and Toni Morris

THREE DIARIES
ACT ONE

JANET, BARRY, and LAWRENCE speak what they are writing in their diaries. At other times, they speak to themselves, act out what they do and say with imaginary characters, speak as other characters, and speak directly to audience members. They mime most actions without props.

A spot rises on BARRY, writing in his diary.

BARRY: Friday, September 5, 1986. Dear diary, the most beautiful woman in all of Asheville stepped into Lloyd's Grocery.

(JANET steps into a second light and writes a check.)

JANET: Lloyd's Grocery. One hundred twenty dollars and forty-one cents. Thank you, Mr. Lloyd. You can have a bag boy take these to my car.

(BARRY rushes to the grocery scene.)

BARRY: I'll carry those for you.
JANET: Oh ... Uh, thank you.
(She walks a few steps into a dimly lit area and freezes in place, keeping her back to BARRY.)

BARRY: No, I think she said more than that.
JANET: Oh, thank you for your kindness.
BARRY: Or maybe ...
JANET: Thank you for ... for looking into my eyes. You see my pain.
BARRY: That was it! Or maybe even—
JANET: Don't let anyone know we feel this way for one another. Our secret.

1

(She walks into a light and is stopped by BARRY.)

BARRY: Oh Miss?
JANET: Yes?
BARRY: Your license plate? K-E-N-N-Y, Kenny. Is that your name?

(JANET frowns and exits.)

BARRY: What if Kenny isn't her name? What if it's her husband's name? I'd hate him, making her drive around, wearing his name. We must not hurt Kenny.
(He sits and writes.)
I will wait for your second message, most beautiful woman. Barry Grotsky.

(Lights fade on BARRY, rise on JANET, sitting and writing.)

JANET: Friday, September 5, 1986. Dear diary, Dr. Mansfield ordered that I get out of the house. Do something. Anything. So, I went out. Lloyd's Grocery. Uneventful. Except a young man looked at my license plate, asked if my name was Kenny. Driving away I thought, is that who I am? Mrs. Franklin Kenny? I had my own name. Janet Holmes. Assigned by my parents. Now who? Mom? But with the twins at boarding school, I'm not "Mom" either ... Once again, Etta Mae transgressed her maid position and scolded me for shopping alone. "Miss Kinny, you plum crazy." She introduced me to her baby brother, whom Franklin hired for yard work. Now who have I become? House manager?

(A light rises on LAWRENCE. JANET steps into it.)

LAWRENCE: Nice to meet you ma'am.

JANET: Nice to meet you, LJ. Etta has said pleasant things about your work.

LAWRENCE: Lawrence. Only Etta calls me LJ.

JANET: Lawrence. Well, Etta? I'll let you put my coat away. *(She exits.)*

LAWRENCE: Hush, Etta! I already promise I ain't gonna drink nothin' workin' here. You ain't my mama.

(Lights dim on LAWRENCE, rise on JANET, writing.)

JANET: Dear diary, with the twins away, our home lost energy ... Franklin called to say Martha and Wallace will join us for sailing in Grenada. Thank goodness we'll have a yacht with three heads. Last year, they dominated both heads by themselves.

(Lights fade on JANET, rise on LAWRENCE, writing.)

LAWRENCE: Dear diary, Etta is the best sister in the world even though she got a big preachin' mouth. But I keep my promise. I won't drink none. Lawrence J. Greene.

(Lights fade on LAWRENCE, rise on BARRY, writing.)

BARRY: Dear diary, Mr. Lloyd sent me to deliver food to Asheville's most fancy restaurant. French. "Jaw it new it." Uh, "Zur a knee." Anyways, I never ate in a French cafe before.
(Walks to restaurant.)
Wow. Real white roses on the tables. I like that Spanish lady with that expensive-dressed man. Look at her. She handed him one'a the white roses. I don't like him. But, I could fall in love with her. I won't. I gotta save myself for that most beautiful woman.

3

(Lights fade on BARRY, rise on JANET, lighting a candle at home. Her phone rings and she answers.)

JANET: Don't bother to say it. You'll be late. Business.

(She hangs up, blows out candle, and sips martini.)

(LAWRENCE enters.)

JANET: LJ? Uh, Lawrence?
LAWRENCE: Yes, Miss Kinny?
JANET: Could you build a fire in the study? Mr. Kenny won't be home for this splendid moussaka. Help yourself to it.
LAWRENCE: Yes ma'am. I mean, thank you, ma'am.
JANET: I'll dine on this martini.
LAWRENCE: I'll git some'a that cedar wood out 'hind the garage. Cedar fires smell real good.
JANET: There are additional logs out by the old stone wall.
LAWRENCE: I seen them blood spots on that wall. Etta say it's devil's blood.
JANET: Horse blood from a mishap in the 1800s.
LAWRENCE: You gonna be alone tonight, Miss Kinny?
JANET: That's standard in this house. Franklin is obsessed with designing grand sailboats.
LAWRENCE: Whatever you say, Miss Kinny.

(He exits. JANET writes.)

JANET: Dear diary. Now I am the yacht builder's aging wife who dines alone. Drinks alone. Passes out alone.

(Lights fade on JANET, rise on BARRY as he sneaks into a store with a flashlight.)

4

BARRY: If Mr. Lloyd catches me opening his cash register, I'm dead.
(He thumbs through the cash register contents.)
Here's her check. "Kenny." "Franklin and Janet Kenny." Janet.
(He kisses check.)
"North Carolina driver's license 7583574." Your phone number ends, "08." My birthday's the 8th. Lander's Lane. I'll get a map.

(Lights fade on BARRY, rise on LAWRENCE.)

LAWRENCE: Look at all them mear-rows. I ain't that bad lookin'. Don't matter none what Mama and Etta say. It's a fact. I be a cool lookin' dude.

(JANET laughs and talks in the dark.)

JANET: Don't baby talk so loudly. Someone will hear ... I don't need another "drinkie first," and I am not building another tee-pee with you.
(She howls as Franklin would howl like a wolf.)
Shhh. Our new help will hear you.
LAWRENCE: *(Calls out to JANET.)* Miss Kinny you okay in there? I heared a dog howl.
JANET: Oh my God. No, Lawrence. Just uh ... We're fine. Thank you, Lawrence.
(She muffles her laughter and whispers.)
See what you did. I need one of my Valiums.

(LAWRENCE walks to another area, talks as self and Etta.)

LAWRENCE: Etta git mad at me. Tode me to never go up no stairs in this house. I tode her I heared somethin' peculiar like a wolf.

"What wuz you doin' upstairs, LJ?"

"Jest lookin' at them mear-rows. On the ceilin'. On the walls. That dumpster I used to hide in 'hind Mr. Kirk's Seafood Restaurant? Smelt like vomik. Steve Fattelo give me drugs. Made it look like a castle. But this place, Etta? I swear I really be in a castle."

"LJ? You is crazy, child. Jest like Mama said you wuz."

"Mama wuz the crazy one. Gittin' drugged up in bed with her men."

Etta slapped me.

"Never talk bad 'bout Mama agin. Now, go walk the Kinny's dog and learn to be useful."

I am useful. I ain't crazy. No matter what ignorant people say.

(Exits, calling for dog.)

Horatio? Here boy.

(JANET enters light, talking to audience.)

JANET: Daddy invited me to DC to see his newly decorated senate office. I'm disinclined to go. Claims he and Mother followed my sketches "to a T." "Your designs are clever, Janet baby. Elegant in the style of the summer flats we engaged in London."

"Daddy? Your sincerity is leaky as the Titanic."

"Well doll baby, get out! Do something nice for others. Those lovely flowers in your green house. Give one to the mailman, one to Etta, one to that new yard boy."

(She passes out flowers to different people.)

Etta, a mum for you ...

(LAWRENCE steps into light.)

6

JANET: A red mum for you, Lawrence.

LAWRENCE: Wy that be real nice, Miss Kinny. I put it in a mason jar in the sunshine like mama done with her little violets ... Etta? Don't look at me like that. Mama done nice thin's once in a while.

(Lights fade on LAWRENCE, rise on BARRY, wearing an apron. JANET walks to store.)

JANET: A mum for you Mr. Lloyd, a mum for your butcher, for your bread and pastry chefs, for your bag boys.

(She hands a mum to BARRY, takes a few steps into a dimly lit area and freezes, her back to BARRY.)

BARRY: Your second message! Friday, September 12th. I shall remember Friday, September 12th long as I live. Janet Kenny, Janet of Landers. From your garden. Your hand picked it for me.

JANET: So, you understand my message?

BARRY: I'm trying.

JANET: The mum, the mum. I cut it free.

BARRY: The mum was a prisoner?

JANET: Like me.

BARRY: My poor Janet.

JANET: What's the plan?

BARRY: I don't have a plan.

JANET: With no plan, the deepest love this world could know? Will wither.

(She steps into the dark. BARRY pulls off his apron.)

BARRY: Mr. Lloyd, I'm sorry, but I gotta quit. There are times when a man has to have a plan.

(BARRY exits as lights rise on JANET.)

JANET: Dear diary, I eavesdropped on Daddy and Franklin. Daddy talked about making another donation to Franklin. Franklin asked if they were working for the right side. Daddy answered rather strongly, "Do I need to remind you how much our arrangement is boosting your little yacht company?"

(Lights fade on JANET, rise on LAWRENCE.)

LAWRENCE: I like them mear·rows. I don't care what Etta say. I ain't ugly.
(Low pitch.)
"Hi LJ."
(High pitch.)
Hi, Mr. Hudson.
(He slaps himself. Low pitch.)
"LJ, you a handsome child, come here, boy, and let Ramont show you how cigars burn."
(High pitch.)
No, Mr. Hudson.
(Low pitch.)
"You little runt. Let's see that little itsy, bitsy thing you got down there."
(He slaps himself. High pitch, crying.)
Stop him, Mama.
(Mid pitch.)
"LJ, you listen to what Ramont say."
(High pitch.)
No, Mama, no.
(Strange voice.)
<u>Punish her God, more times! Burn her God!</u>
(Whispering.)
I best git downstairs.
(Looks up at a shelf.)

Wait! What's on that top shelf?
(*He steps onto a stool, looks on shelf, retrieves pistol.*)
A gun. Mr. Kinny got hisself a gun.
(*He places pistol back on shelf.*)
I won't take Mr. Kinny's gun. I leave it be.

(*Lights fade on LAWRENCE, rise on JANET, sitting at breakfast table, talking with Franklin.*)

JANET: (*Irritated.*) Yes, Franklin, Daddy was one-hundred percent correct. People liked my mums ... Yes! I am taking my antidepressant. Satisfied?
(*Sips coffee. Ponders a moment.*)
I miss Jonathan and James. I know you believe we are obliged to share them with the world, but I preferred when they were exclusively my treasures.

(*She swallows a pill, washes it down with a drink, moves to another area, and writes in diary.*)

JANET: Dear diary, Franklin announced plans to run for mayor of Asheville. He's reorganizing his yacht firm, delegating responsibilities. He won't have to fly to the coast so often. I read his press release. Eloquent. Too eloquent. Someone must have written it for him. I sleep next to that man every night and still have little idea who he is.

(*She swallows another pill, follows with a drink, and talks to audience.*)

JANET: Daddy was ecstatic with Franklin's mayoral decision. Volunteered Mother's help. Invitations, organizing dinners, floral arrangements. Then dictated what I must do.

"Throw a little benefit like I did for that Costa Rica Student Exchange Program. Pepper it with an international flavor."
Really? International? Mayor of Ashville?
"Aim for the future. Right Franklin, my boy?"
Daddy suggested I set up a fund raiser for Asheville's homeless—I didn't know Asheville had homeless.
"Mingling with public folks is always a plus."
Daddy pulled Etta and Lawrence aside.
"Etta? Lawrence my boy? When you're out there with common people, say lots'a good things. Let them know that we are one big happy family."

(LAWRENCE steps into the light.)

LAWRENCE: Wy yes sir, Mr. Senator. I say the best stuff you ever heared! And I washed your limo so good you see yer face in it, sir.

JANET: Excuse me. I think I'll catch some fresh mountain air.

(Lights fade on LAWRENCE as JANET steps onto porch, drinks, and stares at sky.)

JANET: Two decades I watched that gold autumn moon rise over Marble Hill, lighting tombstones against the dark. Every month a new moon. One night that moon's going to get punctured by the branches of that big birch's strong limbs, plunge into the cemetery. There'll be a little tombstone with one word chiseled on it, "moon." Franklin's baby is a sailboat, a mayor's race. I could have had more babies. Franklin said, no.

(Lights rise on BARRY, sitting on the ground, looking through binoculars at JANET.)

BARRY: I see you looking up at this hill for me, Janet girl. That's a third message. Wow. Your house is a palace. Landers Palace, Janet of Landers Palace.
(He writes in diary.)
Dear diary. Tonight, sitting on Marble Hill, I feel inches from Janet. When she searched for me, I felt smaller than small, like I was inside her. Love forever, Barry.

(Lights fade on BARRY and JANET, rise on LAWRENCE, sitting on the ground, writing.)

LAWRENCE: Dear God, my back pain wuz so bad I drunk the gin. I only meant to sip it, I swear. I be hidin' 'neath the garage so Mr. Kinny don't find me.
(He slaps at his ear.)
Darn flies git in my ears.
(He looks at ground beside him.)
What's that? ... Is that you, Horatio? Wake up boy. It's me, LJ.
(He pokes with finger, trying to arouse dog.)

(JANET yells from dark.)

JANET: Horatio? Here puppy. Horatio?
LAWRENCE: Is you dead? You's dead ain't ya? Etta'll blame me if they find you dead 'neath here. I never killt no poor little puppy jest wantin' love. God? Don't let Etta blame me.

(Lights fade on LAWRENCE, rise on BARRY, still on ground, looking in a dictionary.)

BARRY: I have my Webster's with me, because I pressed your mum inside it. The "J" section. "Janet." Between "Janesville, Wisconsin, population 35,164" and "jangle."

"Janet" ... pronounced with French accent, Juh·naa.
"French psychologist, died 1947." Huh! Now that's a
coincidence, huh old girl. 1947. Bet that was about the
time you were born.

*(LAWRENCE enters BARRY'S territory, carrying empty
trash bag and shovel.)*

BARRY: Hey!

LAWRENCE: *(Startles.)* Oh my gosh. You scared me so bad I
'most messed my pants.

BARRY: You work for the Kennys.

LAWRENCE: Yard boy, maybe.

BARRY: What are you doing up here in this cemetery?

LAWRENCE: Buryin' somethin', maybe.

BARRY: Something?

LAWRENCE: Cat I found maybe.

BARRY: The Kenny's cat?

LAWRENCE: Maybe a stray.

BARRY: They got kids?

LAWRENCE: Guess so. Twins. Boys.

BARRY: They at home?

LAWRENCE: I ain't seen'em.

BARRY: You like working for'em?

LAWRENCE: It's one big, happy family. Mr. Senator let me
polish his limo and play in the back with his TV. Has a
little bar but I don't touch his drinks none. 'Specially no
gin.

BARRY: Expensive gin?

LAWRENCE: I gotta be goin'. Nice to make your
acquaintance.

BARRY: What's your name, acquaintance?

LAWRENCE: Lawrence James Greene. Etta jest call me, LJ.

BARRY: Well LJ, nice to make your acquaintance. I'm Barry.

LAWRENCE: You up here by yerself?

BARRY: Star watching. I'm used to being alone.

LAWRENCE: Me, too.

BARRY: I was alone in a hospital for seven months.

LAWRENCE: I wuz in the 'mergency room a couple'a times.

BARRY: My school bus backed over me. I was six. Seven months in the hospital. Two years at home in bed.

LAWRENCE: I ain't never been in bed that long.

BARRY: Grandmother Grotsky used to read Russian fairy tales to me. Promised she'd take me out to eat caviar and drink Russian vodka.

LAWRENCE: I like vodka, but I don't touch it none.

BARRY: She had a stroke. Two years we were in the same room laying in twin beds. Me in casts and braces, Grandmother Grotsky stuck in her dying body. That must be the worst. Stuck inside yourself.

LAWRENCE: Sometimes I git stuck, can't git out.

BARRY: The doctors said she didn't know anything. She knew. I saw inside her. The Kenny's stone wall? Big limos? My eyes see right through them.

LAWRENCE: Well, okay, can I go now?

BARRY: It's a free country, LJ.

LAWRENCE: Nice to make your acquaintance.

(He exits.)

BARRY: *(To self.)* Nice to make your acquaintance, too, Lawrence James Greene.

(Lights fade on BARRY, rise on JANET, writing.)

JANET: Dear diary, Franklin presented me Mother's list. Church services and PTA meetings to visit. I asked Daddy's pilots to fly me up to Exeter to visit the twins. Franklin disapproved. Cancelled my flight.
"You can't fly off in the middle of my campaigning. Our sons don't need a doting mother stunting their growth."

13

As if his mother didn't dote on him. She holds the record for the number of boxes of cakes and cookies a mother can mail. Not to mention pink, perfumed stationary. It was a miracle she let him travel with me our senior year. *(She walks as reminisces.)*
We hiked from Alaska up into the Yukon. Chilkoot Pass. Cold, wet. Found where an old mining town once stood. Rusted bed springs covered in wildflowers ... Franklin proposed.
(Laughs.)
I thought he had smoked too much mary jane. Was going to take me right there on those bedsprings ... Our spot. Magical. Light, wind, color, shadow ... Love, marijuana, setting sun turning gorge walls red-orange, cliffs reaching up like a cathedral. Other worldly. Atop the cliff, a Tlingit child's voice echoed a simple Slavic hymn. A trickle of energy up the back of my neck, a chilly run over my shoulders, across my arms. Millions of micro goose bumps exploding in orgasm.

(LAWRENCE discretely steps onto porch.)

LAWRENCE: Miss Kinny? Sorry to disturb you, ma'am, but Etta Mae say Miss Celia's on the phone. Got herself a crisis wantin' to know if you gonna sponsor that white guy from South Africa that writes black people plays?
JANET: Mr. Fugard. Thank you, Lawrence. Inform Etta I'll return Miss Celia's call.
LAWRENCE: Yes, ma'am.

(Lights fade on LAWRENCE and JANET, rise on BARRY, knocking at front door. LAWRENCE answers it.)

LAWRENCE: Etta can't come to the door. What'chu want?
BARRY: I'm volunteering to buy groceries at Mr. Lloyd's from now on for Mrs. Kenny.

LAWRENCE: You that strange Barry boy up in the cemetery. No sir. Miss Kinny don't need no shoppin'. That there's my sister Etta's job.
(He closes door.)

(BARRY sees a magazine on the porch table and opens it.)

BARRY: Beautiful women in cigarette ads. Prisoners in their bodies, staring out at readers. Not as beautiful as you Janet of Lander's. They won't let you grocery shop, huh? Who took you from me, buried you in the pit of your own body? You need protecting? I'll protect. That's me, "The Protector."

(Lights fade on BARRY, rise on LAWRENCE.)

LAWRENCE: Mix a little water in with the gin. Nobody know no difference.
(Startles.)
Etta! You jest made my heart jump out ... Nothin'. Jest dustin' bottles off. Mindin' my own business like other folk should do ... I ain't stealin' no liquor off a the Kinnys. Now leave me be ... Horatio? Ain't see'im ... Now, wy you ask me twiced if'n the first time I say I ain't seen'im? You'd blame me fer it rainin' ... Don't call me retard!

(LAWRENCE exits and re-enters another lit area.)

LAWRENCE: I kin read'n write. Mama tode Etta never call me dumb!
(In strange voice.)
<u>I don't know nothin' you bitch and I don't have to take yer mess and you can stuff it down yer mouth you whore with those fatso smelly bastards Mama drug home callin' me names and I kill all'a you and puke on you!</u>

15

(He writes, still speaking in strange voice.)
<u>And if you lay a hand on Etta agin I swear I kill you.</u>
<u>Larry!</u>

(Lights fade on LAWRENCE, rise on JANET, talking on phone.)

JANET: *(Rambling.)* And while your father's trotting on the campaign trail, Celia and I are enveloped by this homeless benefit, telephoning florists and caterers and musicians. You know how I hate being in public and ... Oh, honey. What kind of nightmare?
(She paces while listening.)
Listen! Do not tell James about your nightmare. He takes after your father. He'll make fun of you ... I'm just warning you.
(She writes.)
Dear diary, John called, described a memory when he, James, and their Uncle Max went shopping in South Africa. John stayed in the car—as usual. A black woman on the street smiled at him. Without warning, a group of Africaners hit her with pipes, walked away laughing. She sat up, pulled her skirt down over her knees proper like, like nothing happened. But John saw blood trickle from her ear. Max explained that's the worst sign, blood coming from ears. That memory is now John's nightmare. He said to me, "Mom? I'm sorry for that time I broke your crystal sugar bowl." I told him, "There will be no more nightmares. I'll borrow them from you, like I used to do when you were little."
(She startles as Franklin enters.)
Gracious! It's not funny, Franklin, for you to sneak up on me ... Apology accepted. I guess ... What?! For a mayor's race in small city, North Carolina? No! I absolutely forbid having security guards. Tell Daddy that's not acceptable.

(Lights fade on JANET, *rise on* BARRY, *watching the Kennys' house through binoculars.)*

BARRY: Janet of Landers. I memorized every line of your house. Six chimneys stretch to the sky like an insect dying on its back. Cool fall air, yet no smoke from your chimneys. Maybe you have electric heat. Little dials exactly controlling temperature. Like hospital dials. More oxygen. Less oxygen. Faster breaths. Slower breaths.
(Looks around.)
I like this cemetery.
(Reads grave marker.)
"Reverend Paul Anderson and his beloved wife Rebecca."
(He sniffs the ground.)
Damp earth. Love made eternal by death. We gotta die, Janet. People will forever say our names together. "Janet Kenny and Barry Grotsky." An eternal couple.

(Lights fade on BARRY, *rise on* LAWRENCE.)*

LAWRENCE: Don't go bein' "mad as mess" at me, Etta Mae Greene. I ain't gotta come home at night if'n I don't want. I got my own place thank you very much. I come'n go as I please. Ain't gotta tell nobody nothin'.

(JANET enters, dressing.)

JANET: Etta, can you hook these pearls for me?
(Turns her back for Etta to hook necklace.)
LAWRENCE: Them sure are purty, Miss Kinny.
JANET: Thank you, Lawrence.

(JANET walks to desk in another light and writes as lights fade on LAWRENCE.)*

JANET: Dear diary, Franklin introduced our mandated security guards, Agents Charles Portego and Philip Spinoza. Mr. Portego was holding pieces of Aunt Geraldine's Chicago World's Fair Lamp. Unable to see— since he wore sunglasses inside—he shattered it. He offered a pathetically insincere apology and Franklin recklessly accepted. "That's far more than that dinosaur lamp deserves."
I chimed in, "I imagine it's difficult to avoid sentimental antiques when you elect to wear spyglasses inside."
The agent removed his glasses.

(LAWRENCE steps into the light.)

JANET: Franklin introduced our help. "Gentlemen? This is Lawrence and Etta Greene, our landscape foreman and house affairs advisor."
LAWRENCE: I'm jest the yard boy. Etta's baby brother, not no husband or nothin' like that ... Now how's they gonna know that, Etta, if I don't tell'em?

(LAWRENCE exits as the lights lower to a dim glow. JANET circles a spot-lit area, as if examining Charles.)

JANET: Agent Charles Portego. Muscular, mysterious, eye glow the color of an Alaskan Malamute. I wonder if beneath that uniform of polyester, Charles wears boxers or as the twins say, squeezers. Golly. Am I old enough this well-trained source of authority seems like a play thing? One light mole on his right ear lobe. No wedding band. I melt in this young man's eyes.
(She circles a second spot-lit area, examining Franklin.)
Like I see you swoon, Franklin, your eyes ingesting silly young women. Once upon a time, you and I had the

combined vision of a mighty cyclops, missing nothing. But we built walls.
(She walks to audience.)
This afternoon, security guard Agent Charles Portego smashed Aunt Geraldine's Chicago World's Fair Lamp. And I felt a rush of life.

(Lights fade on JANET, rise on BARRY, sitting on a blanket and writing.)

BARRY: Dear People of the World, I sneaked into Mom's apartment and took the quilt Grandmother Grotsky stitched. I stole oranges from Mr. Lloyd's, the first time I ever stole, well, except for Janet's check, but I paid back the cash register for that. Now, I appreciate how difficult it was for her to send messages to me. Rich ladies like her don't shop or write checks. How else could she let me know? Thanks, babe. Laying here on Marble Hill, near your house, is the most peace I've known. Barry and Janet. The Liberator and Janet of Landers. That turns me on. A guy's gotta relieve himself if you get my drift, princess.

(He lies on blanket and massages his abdomen, oblivious JANET and Charles are approaching.)

JANET: Agent Portego?
(Turns to look at valley, out of breath.)
Look at that. Premium view of the valley. Always comforts me ... I hoped Horatio would be up here. Our twins used to bring him here. Play space wars ... Disrespectful?
(Laughs.)
Playing war in a cemetery? Ah. You and Daddy share the same play book. Not me. I encouraged my boys to play

"shoot'em up" on this hill. Where better than a cemetery to learn connections of war and death?

BARRY: *(Startled.)* What!

JANET: Oh, pardon us ... Surely, you aren't camping here in a cemetery.

BARRY: I wanted to get away from city lights last night. Star watch. Orion, Venus.

JANET: Oh. Well, we're searching for a black and white dog. Not much larger than a cat. Answers to, "Horatio."

BARRY: Horatio? Nope. No Horatio here.

(JANET walks, stopping to speak to audience.)

JANET: On the way down the slope, my assigned guard said a most unkind thing. "In high school, that wierdo's the kind of person we called, 'science nerd.'" I lost all interest in Agent Portego.
(She exits.)

BARRY: Never in my wildest dreams did I think you would come to me. Who were me and you in previous lives? I bet novels and love poems were written about us.
(He kneels by a tombstone.)
"Paul and Rebecca. 1823." Probably buried in pine coffins. Praying heavy ground will soften and splinter the wood. Set them free. These days people are trapped in air-tight metal caskets. Nothing comes in or gets out. Janet, my love, we must find a better way to remain together. Hang in there, babe.

(Lights fade on BARRY, rise on LAWRENCE.)

LAWRENCE: No sir, Mr. Kinny sir, I never stole no gin bottles ... No siree. I don't know nothin' 'bout nothin' like that, sir. Ain't watered down yer gin. Maybe some kids busted in and done it. You ain't gonna say nothin' to Etta 'bout this, is you?

(Lights fade on LAWRENCE, rise on JANET, talking to audience.)

JANET: In church, Daddy was in prototypal form, shaking hands, clarifying why Franklin was absent from church. "Cutting a ribbon for a new hospital wing. Political harvests come from careful baby kissing." And then to my chagrin, I babbled, "Oh, no, no, Becky Lee. My parents are merely visiting us this weekend. Franklin has no inkling of running for Congress. Goodness Becky Lee Winston, you act like our family's full of the biggest manipulators this side of Raleigh. Now go donate more of your family's money for that hospital wing." God, I hate when I sound like Mother.
(Turns and speaks to another church woman.)
"Florence Robins? How sweet you look with that tiny peacock feather hat. You are coming to our house Wednesday night for that little teeny-weeny fund raiser, aren't you?" Oh. My. Gosh.

(Lights fade on JANET, rise on BARRY and LAWRENCE, talking at front door.)

LAWRENCE: No, Mr. Kinny do all his own hirin' and he ain't here, so you best go downtown to his offices if you serious 'bout workin' fer'im. But he ain't said nothin' 'bout needin' nobody.
BARRY: Please help me. I'm a friend of Janet Kenny—And you.
LAWRENCE: I ain't got no friends. 'Specially not you. And Miss Kinny sure ain't no friend'a yers.
BARRY: I gotta see Mr. Kenny. I need a job.

LAWRENCE: As Etta say, "Jest another bum lookin' fer work."

(BARRY peers around LAWRENCE.)

BARRY: Wait! I saw Mr. Kenny.
(Yells.)
Mr. Kenny?! Mr. Kenny?!

(LAWRENCE turns and looks behind him, then back to BARRY.)

LAWRENCE: That ain't Mr. Kinny. That's our security man. Mr. Charles.
BARRY: No. The man who walked by. <u>That</u> was Mr. Kenny. I saw him at the French restaurant where I deliver bread and fruit. He was with a real pretty Spanish lady.

(LAWRENCE turns and answers Charles.)

LAWRENCE: Oh. Mr. Charles. Yes sir. This here is Barry, sir. Barry? This here is Mr. Charles.
BARRY: Mr. Charles? ... Oh, sorry. Agent Portego. I'm a friend of Mrs. Kenny and LJ here.
LAWRENCE: He ain't no friend'a mine.
BARRY: I met you and Mrs. Kenny two days ago up where I was camping. I came here to get a job with Mr. Kenny ... Sir? ... Yes sir. I saw both of'em at the French restaurant.
(Slowly, carefully.)
"Zur a knee." Something like that. French. White roses on the tables ... Yes sir. I'm positive he was there. Mr. Kenny with a Spanish woman. Looked Spanish ... Shoot yeah! I'll be glad to talk with you and Mr. Kenny ... In the library? Fantastic!
(BARRY walks away with Charles, still talking.)
I've been wanting to see the inside of this mansion.

LAWRENCE: I swear. 'Nother bum lookin' fer work.

(Lights fade on LAWRENCE, rise on Barry, writing in cemetery.)

BARRY: Dear people of the world. After studying Franklin Kenny and his sun-glassed prison guard in the library, it's obvious they only want Janet Kenny for her body. They imprison her heart. Well, a plan is in the making. "The Liberator."

(Lights dim on BARRY, rise on LAWRENCE.)

LAWRENCE: Shut up Etta! I kin come in Mr. Kinny's bar room if and when I want. I tode you I ain't gonna drink. Ain't gonna jeopardize yer job. Good night!
(He watches Etta leave, speaks under breath.)
Yeah. You jest go do that ... Mr. Kinny promised me he ain't gonna say nothin' to Etta. He lied.
(Strange voice.)
Ass lickin' liar.

(Lights fade on LAWRENCE, rise on JANET, writing in diary, intoxicated.)

JANET: Dear diary, Daddy called me into the library, under the pretense Franklin had good news to share, but it turns out, our so-called security people turned up damaging—painfully damaging news.

(Lights rise on BARRY in cemetery and LAWRENCE under garage, remaining on all three people for a collage of on-going conversations and monologues.)

23

BARRY: I must be clever. Killing is wrong, but so is suffering.

LAWRENCE: Etta ask me about Horatio agin and about the gin agin, and I know she not be trustin' me no more and—

(Strange voice.)

<u>I did not lie, you bitch! I don't have to take none'a yer mess. You stuff it down yer mouth.</u>

JANET: A woman ... A beautiful Spanish woman.

BARRY: My dearest Janet, it is not your death or mine that will unite us eternally.

LAWRENCE: I dug up Horatio. Thought he'd be bones, but his funny little ears still stick up. I like to vomik when bugs crawl outta his eye.

JANET: Rendezvous, restaurants, hotels. Franklin tried to explain.

(Franklin's voice.)

"She sought me out. Strictly business. It was never sexual."

(Her own voice.)

Daddy asked him to move out.

BARRY: We must keep our intimacy secret. They want you for your beauty, and you are beautiful, but they cannot see your heart.

LAWRENCE: *(Strange voice.)* <u>You whore and fatso smelly bastards you drug home callin' me names and slappin' Etta and I kill you if you blame me fer stealin' gin.</u>

(He crawls out from under garage.)

JANET: Not sexual! What then? Sharing private secrets of your soul? You claim, "Business. Charity." Lies, Franklin!

BARRY: Franklin Kenny's weak. When I stared in his eyes, he flinched. He has razor nicks about his neck, the sign of an unsteady hand.

LAWRENCE: I never see Etta so happy as takin' care'a sick folk. Singin', "When the Saints Go Marching In." Puttin' out Miss Kinny's pills fer her.

JANET: I hit Franklin with my fists. Hit him again. Etta ran for my pills, but I knew what I needed. A drink. And another.

LAWRENCE: I moved poor little Horatio down by the river. Rain'll wash him downstream.

JANET: Daddy threatened Franklin.

(Senator's voice.)

"I can put up with anything except you risking my daughter and grandsons. By the time this clears, you bastard, you'll wish you were dead!"

(Taking pills from Etta.)

Thank you, Etta.

(Swallows pills and drinks.)

Etta said,

(Etta's voice.)

"Dr. Mansfield warned us, bad mixin'em martinis with them medicines, Miss Kinny. You go plum crazy."

(Her own voice.)

I'm already crazy, Etta.

(She walks to closet, stands on chair, searches top shelf as talks.)

I love Etta's simple philosophies.

(Etta's voice.)

"Boys are angel's choirs. Growed up men, Satan's work. Women spoils little boys, then they grow up and cheat and be beasts led around by their privates. I say, do away with'em all."

(Her own voice.)

Good going, girl ... Oh God, Franklin's yelling at Lawrence again about watering down his gin. Glad he doesn't know I diluted it.

(Continues searching closet shelf.)

25

DC Fidler

Where is it?

(LAWRENCE kneels in a tight-ball posture and rocks.)

LAWRENCE: Etta say bad things 'bout me and I hate her.
(Strange voice.)
I hate Mr. Kinny, God. Punish him!
JANET: Where the hell is that lying bastard's gun?
LAWRENCE: *(Strange voice.)* Run a pole up him. Wiggle it
'round. I won't care. He lies. Fill him with the nastiest
filth 'til he splodes and make him hurt 'til he thinks he's
gonna rip in two!
JANET: Where are you hiding, little pistol? ... Ah. There you
are.
*(She finds pistol, covers her hand with handkerchief,
picks up pistol, and stares at it.)*

BARRY: Men treat women badly, so we must sacrifice Mr.
Kenny to teach lessons. God will forgive me, because I do
this for the world. Children smile because of the love of
the Sacrificer for Janet of Landers. "The Sacrificer."

INTERMISSION

26

THREE DIARIES
ACT TWO

Spot rises on JANET in bed, still intoxicated, writing in her diary. She swallows a pill and drinks.

JANET: This morning Daddy woke me with words that crushed my soul. "The police said it looks like a tragic accident. Too much to drink and he fell into the pool."

(Lights rise on LAWRENCE, writing.)

LAWRENCE: They pull Mr. Kinny outta his swimmin' pool. Make a big fuss. Now he kin never tell Etta lies about me. I am sorry he is dead, but it will help me lots. Etta will be in a good way helpin' Miss Kinny. I heared her say when she seen Mr. Kinny floatin', everybody'll be better off. Lawrence J. Greene.
(He walks to another light, talks to audience, worried.)
I hear Etta screamin' real bad. All them policemans run to her 'partment.

(Lights fade on LAWRENCE.)

JANET: Dr. Mansfield insists I continue my medication. No more martinis ... Mother said the twins already boarded Daddy's plane and should be here for dinner. If I sober up, I am told, I shall be "permitted" to ride with them to the airport. Whoopee.

(Phone rings and she answers.)

JANET: John? ... Oh, James ... You already landed? I was supposed to meet you two ... Oh ... Well, the police think he hit his head on the pool wall ... Yeah. An excellent swimmer. But he had been drinking.

(Lights fade on JANET, rise on BARRY, sitting on quilt on ground.)

BARRY: October 28, 1986. Dear women of the world, you are pure and I release you from your prisons. You are the center of what is glorious. Angels of the universe, I deliver you into meadows of happiness. You are my flock. You will dwell in this love that came from sacrifice. Lust not, but know one another. This I command or you will fall beneath the sword of the almighty. Your Savior.

(Lights fade on BARRY, rise on LAWRENCE, walking to JANET.)

LAWRENCE: *(Wiping dirt off pants.)* Miss Kinny? Etta tode me to tell you, since she don't feel good right now, them policemans done finish takin' photographs, dustin' fer fingerprints and junk. If you care to move back in yer room, she done with fixin' it up.
JANET: Thank you, Lawrence, but I feel safer in the twins' room.
LAWRENCE: Etta say they be comin' back today.
JANET: I'll wait for them here. Thank you, Lawrence.
LAWRENCE: Yes ma'am ... Etta say they find Horatio somehow. He dead. Sorry. She say to fetch all yer liquor and take'em down to the cellar—

(When LAWRENCE reaches for her drink, JANET grabs it.)

JANET: Don't!
LAWRENCE: Land's sakes. I best go.

(LAWRENCE exits.)

JANET: *(Drunkenly mumbles.)* Thank you, Lawrence.

(Lights fade on JANET, rise on LAWRENCE as he crawls under garage.)

LAWRENCE: Too many policemans and mad people. I fear fer my life. I best stay under here.
(When he sees Charles stoop to look under the garage house, he leans and looks back at him.)
Hey, Mr. Charles ... Fine, sir ... No sir. I like it under here ... No sir. Ain't cold or damp ... Yes sir, might could be how come I keep havin' dirt on my knees ... Most every night ... No sir. Ain't seen nothin' last night ... If you want me to.
(He crawls out and stands.)
Where me and you gonna ride?

(Lights fade on LAWRENCE. A light rises on JANET as a second light rises on BARRY, reading a newspaper.)

BARRY: "City stunned over death of business adventurer Franklin Kenny." Front page again, huh Franklin? "Mr. Kenny allegedly fell into his estate's swimming pool."
JANET: Mother and Daddy seem bizarrely happy over Franklin's death.
BARRY: "Business adventurer," huh? Don't mention how many people had it in for you because of all the pain you caused.
JANET: Franklin's red, firm-bristle toothbrush. A trace of moisture left.
BARRY: People make up good memories for the dead, but truth rises outta the ashes like a tin can that refuses to burn in a camp fire. The hunter thought he covered his tracks but one day, sun illuminates a reflecting bit of tin.

JANET: *(Rubbing arm.)* I don't want this bruise to heal. My last cue to remember you. I could forgive you for anything but leaving us to serve out our lives without you.

BARRY: All you "important" people lie about Franklin. But I shall wash, and blow, and illuminate. People will know truth. "The Illuminator."

(Lights fade on JANET and BARRY, rise on LAWRENCE in jail.)

LAWRENCE: This jail smells like piss! Mr. Charles lie to me. Go fer a little ride in his car. Lies! Make up mess 'bout me. Maybe I done put water in gin bottles, maybe I don't. Ignorant people askin' if I know 'bout a dead dog on Etta's pillow. That be the sickest thin' I ever heared.

(Lights fade on LAWRENCE, rise on JANET, writing.)

JANET: Dear diary, Daddy insisted we not tell the twins about Horatio. The police are doing everything to solve this quickly. Then the bottom fell out. Daddy said the coroner discovered Franklin's shoulder was grazed by a bullet. That he had been knocked unconscious with a blunt instrument ... Being unconscious led to his drowning.
(She walks to audience.)
It feels good to have my babies home.
(She mimes hugging the twins.)
Oh my gosh, it's the best to hug you two. Smell you. Strawberry shampoo and teenage boy sweat.
(She releases them.)
I barely had them to myself when Daddy prompted us, "Take a moment. But folks out there are plenty eager to see you three prized citizens."

John was adorable. Referred to our new agents as "security jerks." Daddy ventured to redirect him.

"You must realize, son, there are unpredictable people out there. People determined to rob us of our sadness, add impurity on top of unbearable grief."

(In a daze, to self.)

We received two obscene phone calls. And a strange letter.

(Lights rise on BARRY, reading from letter as JANET reacts.)

BARRY: "Men and women can now look into one another's eyes and know what the heart speaks. With death people bring flowers and smiles. Not because someone died, but because the right person died at the right moment. Soon, people will forget. Again, prisons will rise inside us. But fear not. I shall never cease illuminating ugly truth. The Illuminator."

(Lights fade on BARRY and JANET, rise on LAWRENCE.)

LAWRENCE: I need a drink so bad I cannot stand it! Etta say my lawyer Mr. Garringer say my prints all over Mr. Kinny's gun. I ain't touched no gun 'cept to look at it. Say my prints all over his shovel, too. I tell Etta, "So! I do yard work." Then she say, "Pieces'a Mr. Kenny's scalp's on that shovel, LJ!"

(He calmly talks to self.)

I ain't put no dead dog on Etta's pillow. A sick lie.

(He dissociates and yells.)

And I hope that policeman and Mommy burn in hell fer laughin' at me bein' mean you nasty whore with yer cheap men pissin' on me burnin' my legs with cigs you gonna die you sick bitch!

(Lights fade on LAWRENCE, rise on BARRY, writing.)

BARRY: Dear women of the world, today, Mom left the TV on the "Only Through Christ" network. The Reverend Wilkes Martin sent me messages. I held onto every one of his words.
(He imitates Wilkes Martin.)
"Only Through Christ. Thank you for comin', thank you for tunin' in, hallelujah. Saved from our flesh."

(Lights fade on BARRY, rise on JANET, writing.)

JANET: The boys dressed handsomely for Franklin's funeral. John cried. James, naturally, like Franklin, was stoic. And Etta? Oh my gosh. She wailed. And after she heard the *Citizen Times* speculated Franklin committed suicide over a ruined political career, she threw a fit.
(Imitates Etta.)
"Folks write stories 'fore they even learnt what's goin' on."
(Her own voice.)
I asked her how Lawrence was holding up in jail. She pitifully whispered,
(Imitates Etta.)
"LJ don't kill Mr. Kinny. All his life, he never harm nothin' or nobody."
(Her own voice.)
The twins asked her if Lawrence was retarded, disturbed—That didn't help—She told them,
(Etta's voice.)
"He might be a tad slow, boys, but his heart is good. Somebody else done them terrible things to yer poor daddy. We gotta learn who."
(Her own voice.)

I'm taking the twins to Gingerbread Acres. I need the quiet of our cabin. I didn't invite Etta, to which she said,
(Etta's voice.)
"Don't look like I'm trusted 'round here no more."
(Pause, her own voice.)
James asked Etta if Horatio was going to the cabin. She didn't know what to answer. I suggested, "Let's not break the news to them just yet." She patronizingly snorted,
(Etta's voice.)
"Uh huh. I see. Lie to'em. Uh huh."
(Pauses, not writing. Her own voice.)
I can't remember ... How severely did Franklin and I fight?

(Lights fade on JANET, rise on BARRY, watching TV.)

BARRY: I watched OTC television all day long again, irritated waiting, hoping for Wilkes to read my letter. He read everybody else's.
(Wilkes' voice in sarcastic tone.)
"Now, here's a letter from Dorita Mae Jones, Billings, Montana. 'Dear Reverend Wilkes, how many bathrooms do you have in your OTC Mansion?' Well Dorita Mae, when I wuz a little boy growin' up outside'a Dillon, South Carolina, I didn't have no indoor plumbin'. I visited my cousin Buddy and when I seen Buddy's indoor toilet, I wuz scared to death. Thought when he bumped that shiny little handle my insides wuz plum gonna be sucked out. Thanks for your kind letter, Dorita Mae. Only Through Christ."
(His own voice.)
Toilets! Outhouses! Really? Read <u>my</u> letter!
(Imitates Wilkes.)
"And here's one from our retired folks stayin' in their motor home in the OTC Campground. A gentleman from

Lassitor, Arkansas, wishing happy birthday to his sister, Gretchin, in Bunkie, Louisiana. Well, happy birthday to you darlin' Gretchin. Only Through Christ."
(His own voice.)
Stupid birthday letters. Read my letter!
(Imitates Wilkes.)
"And y'all remember now, not too late to buy one'a our lovely OTC Condominiums. Invest yer life savin's and live out the rest'a yer sun shiny days here at OTC. Only Through Christ."
(His own voice.)
Ads! Scams! ... And then it happened.
(Imitates Wilkes.)
"Now, here's an interestin' letter. Asheville, North Carolina. 'Dear Wilkes, men and women of the world, never agin will men greed and lust and treat women like possessions. Evil in the past becomes beauty in the future.' Signed, 'The Illuminator.' Well Mr. Illuminator, whoever you are, don't hide like a unnamed disciple of Satan. Come forward. Join us. Only Through Christ."
(His own voice.)
Join you? Sooner than you know, Reverend Wilkes Martin. Sooner than you know.
(He makes gun gesture with finger, fires at TV.)

(Lights fade on BARRY, rise on LAWRENCE.)

LAWRENCE: I might as well be dead. Everybody makin' up lies up 'bout me. If I fess I had Mr. Kinny's gun, nobody's gonna believe me 'bout nothin'. If I killt Mr. Kinny, then I should burn in hell. I could not live knowin' I done such a thin'. Poor little Horatio. He liked to lick my hand, sit by me.

(Lights fade on LAWRENCE, rise on JANET, sitting on the floor, warming by a fire, intoxicated, sipping wine, talking to audience.)

JANET: Daddy knew I wanted to be here at the cabin with only my boys, but he can be brutally persuasive when he believes our lives are in danger. Every London holiday as children, he deluged us with security ... I have to admit, I do like having Charles here. He built us a lovely fire. He asked, as a child, did security make me feel safe.
(Chuckles.)
I told him, "No. They terrified me."
(Serious while lost in thought.)
The only time my world felt safe, was with Nanny Nel. When she sang to us. Fed us her cast-iron wedges of cornbread. Freshly churned butter.
(Pause.)
Then tipsy, carelessly, I insulted Charles. "You probably grew up with butter in plastic tubs." I apologized, but damage done. I uncharacteristically asked him to sit closer. Said, "I won't bite"—I actually said that. His response, "No more wine for you!" He saw my guilt. Told me I deserved to "tie one on."
(Pause.)
It feels good being drunk, numb. Tomorrow? I'll sober up, resume obsessing, what did I do Franklin's last hours ... Guilt I betrayed my sons, lied about Horatio ... I used to be an accurate mirror for them, someone to confirm their inner thoughts. My mind's fallen to a dark place. I need a strong woodsman to smash into this cabin, rescue me ... I leaned on Charles' shoulder. "Maybe you are my strong woodsman." He promptly escorted me to my room. Well hells, bells. Chivalry is alive in Gingerbread Acres.

(Lights fade on JANET, rise on BARRY, watching TV.)

35

BARRY: Grandmother Grotsky used to brag about her "massive" church in Russia. "Strong stone walls to block out the world so people peer into their own hearts." She said brave people search inside, find the eyes of God. Well, she certainly stood up to God. Looked him straight in the eyes. So, he turned her into a statue. A pillar of salt. I lay in that room with her frozen, twisted body. I lay in that room with God.
(Pauses, then imitates Wilkes.)
"Y'all? Look through them windows of our beautiful OTC Chapel. Get that view with your camera, Burt. Through the windows. My wife Sue Lynn's dream OTC Hotel. Where you folks can come stay when you're weary from social sleaze and dirt. A sparkling, Jesus-blessed refuge. Thank you, Burt. Bring that camera back in here to our OTC Choir, our OTC Organist, these lovely people donating blessed-earned money. Now, you folks watchin' at home, mail in those donations, and we'll send you for free, 'OTC Recipes for Christmas', plus an OTC Campground T-shirt. Only Through Christ."
(Violently turns off TV, his own voice to audience.)
Enough! ... God sent a message. Commanded me to be his eyes and hands. It's clear. Janet of Landers locked herself in a self-made prison in order to remain pure for me. Waiting for me to make her world safe. Safe from the greedy Reverend Wilkes Martins of this world. Janet honey, my mission is unmistakable.

(Lights fade on BARRY, rise on LAWRENCE, lying in bed. He sits up, coughs, and rubs arm.)

LAWRENCE: My arm hurts. Etta say they move me to Dorthea Dix Insane Hospital cuz I cut myself. I ain't cut myself. She swears I did in the jailhouse. Sawed my arm with my butter knife. I tode her, "If I done that, then it's too bad I did not die. If I done all them bad things, I deserve to be killt."

(Lights fade on LAWRENCE, rise on JANET, writing.)

JANET: Dear diary. The cabin is a replenishing sanctuary. John is reading, *L'Estranger*, speeding through Franklin's books in the order they are shelved. James befriended our other "security jerk," Philip. They hike, talk in the yard. Far enough away I can't hear. John noted insightfully—creepily insightfully, "James likes Philip; you like Charles." I demanded an explanation. He buried his head in *L'Etranger*. Little jerk. Oh, then Jonathan smartly added, "I tossed yours and Charles' empty wine bottles into the recycle bin."

(Lights fade on JANET, rise on BARRY.)

BARRY: Today, on the bus, I met Darlene Yates from Minneapolis, North Carolina. She's on her way to join the OTC Choir. Every other sentence of hers ends in, "Only Through Christ." She said if she failed OTC Choir tryouts, she'd continue down to Disneyworld, try out for Sleeping Beauty or Minnie Mouse. She asked me to share a motel room. I told her I have my old Cub Scout tent. I wouldn't want Janet to think I shared a motel room with the likes of Darlene Yates.

(Lights fade on LAWRENCE, rise on JANET.)

JANET: Thank you, Charles. I appreciate your helping clean the garage and attic. Mother and Daddy would be horrified. "Security aren't family. Keep those boundaries!" ... The spinning loom? Yes, it is cool. A relic Franklin found at a flea market. Wealthy people

purchasing pasts we never earned. Have you seen the twins? ...
(Chuckles.)
Typical. John reads a novel. James climbs a mountain. He named that little peak, "K6." That's sweet of Philip to climb with him. Wish my life problems could be solved by climbing a mountain ... Charles?
(Pauses to muster bravery.)
Did you uh ... ever see ... the woman?—Franklin's Spanish woman? ... Was she beautiful? Sexual? Sensuous? I have a picture stuck in my head. When I was a girl, Daddy told us about Granddaddy's cotton mill. A young boy—too young to be working—caught his hand on tooth-like hooks, pierced his arm, pulled him into the spinner. He begged for someone to mercifully kill him. Only when his arm was shredded, could they pull him free. Every night I closed my eyes, saw rust spots on blue steel hooks, a vivid snapshot. Now ... I have a Spanish woman snapshot.

(Lights fade on JANET, rise on LAWRENCE, sitting at a table.)

LAWRENCE: I hate sittin' with this glass window 'tween us, Etta. Can't hug, touch nobody. Doc tode me sometimes I write my name, "Lawrence," sometimes "LJ," sometimes other persons, "Larry." And color pictures look like they's colored by other people. I got lots'a people inside me, Etta. Some of'em is sick. Do thin's I don't know 'bout ... It's true, Etta! What Doc Clayton tode me. Makes me talk 'bout what happened with Mama and her whorin' men. Don't go Etta! Catch a later bus!
(He crawls into a ball on the floor and cries.)
There's bad in me! It ain't goin' away 'til I's dead. Mama put it in me and I can't git it out! You jest stood by and—
(Strange voice.)

Didn't do nothin' bitch and hate you cunt and gonna make you find out what real pain is real slow 'til you choke on my spit!

(Lights fade on LAWRENCE, rise on JANET, staring out window.)

JANET: *(Startles.)* Oh! Gracious, Charles. Sorry. Franklin and the twins always ... Oh, well ... the twins love to take advantage of how easily I startle ... I was uh ... watching a deer out the window. Well, actually ... spying a bit on James and Philip. They were sitting on the fence, talking. James began crying, leaned on Philip's shoulder. They've been sitting like that a long time ... No, no. Don't you dare ask him to back off! James would be furious. It's bad enough he stares at me with his accusing eyes. Won't talk ... Then he meets an unknown security agent and ... pours out his heart. You must think me ridiculous. It's fortuitous James found a friend ... You've become a friend to me ... Didn't mean to break protocol again. Sorry.

(Lights fade as JANET steps into another spot and writes.)

JANET: Dear diary, John worries I trust Charles too much. He caught Charles snooping around Franklin's roll-top desk. Twice. Charles made excuses both times. Charles didn't find it, but John showed me Franklin's desk has a secret compartment. The twins old school pictures, worn from Franklin's carrying them in his wallet. Papers, receipts, bills. "Southern Supply and Distribution, four hundred thousand dollars." "Southern Supply and Distribution, one million six thousand dollars." "Nine hundred thousand." Never heard of that company.

(Pause.)
Daddy called to say Lawrence's trial begins in two weeks.
John asked if I believe Lawrence killed his father ... I
don't know.
(Pause.)
Tonight, it was wrong of me, but Daddy and Charles
were on the cabin porch talking close to the window.
*(She tiptoes to window, kneels, eavesdrops, and whispers
to audience.)*
Daddy said, "Powerful people won't understand millions
of dollars being unaccounted for." Charles said, "Franklin
diverted it."—That got Daddy's dandruff up—Charles
attempted to calm him, saying he located a woman from
Colombia, Miss Andrade. I wonder if she was Franklin's
Spanish woman in the restaurant? Charles informed him
that Miss Andrade was the person who persuaded
Franklin to divert money to missions for blankets, food,
medicine.
(She walks away from window.)
Daddy yelled his Congress friends earmarked that
money for guns ... for converting Franklin's yachts into
gunboats. Not third world missions.
(Returns and peeps out window.)
Charles is showing Daddy photographs. Daddy called
them, "Collateral damage." Said his Congress friends
risked their reputations to channel money to fight
Colombian rebels. Now, they want distance between
them and that money ... He's demanding Charles
immediately "take care of" Miss Andrade.
*(She walks from window and sits, stunned, afraid,
trembling.)*
I saw the photographs. Dead women and children.

*(Lights fade on JANET, rise on LAWRENCE, playing on
floor with marbles, singing to self and talking baby talk.)*

LAWRENCE: La-la-lala-la. The big marble hits the weeny marble. Bing!

(He holds marbles like puppets talking to one another, imitating Franklin's voice as he moves his marble, and Janet's voice as he moves her marble.)

LAWRENCE: *(Janet's voice.)* "Oh, Franklin! Damn it! How can you do this to us?"
(Franklin's voice.)
"I'm sorry Janet. I wuz tryin' to do what wuz right."
(Janet's voice.)
"More lies!"
(Franklin's voice.)
"Janet, stop it! Put down that gun."
(Baby-talk voice.)
Bing!
(He hits marbles together.)
Bing bing bing bing.
(He curls up in a defensive position, baby talk.)
No, Mommy, no! I won't wet my bed no more. Don't put me in that hamper! I'm sorry I'm sorry I'm sorry!

(Lights fade on LAWRENCE, rise on BARRY, holding a list.)

BARRY: I've got to stay organized. "Number one, pay KOA campground to camp. Number two, apply for OTC personnel position. Three, buy handgun. Four, get on OTC talk show. Five, shoot Reverend Wilkes Martin. Six, buy ring for Janet. Seven, watch more talk shows. Eight, make more plans if needed."

(Lights fade on BARRY, rise on LAWRENCE. He rapidly hits marbles together, screams, and then talks in a strange voice.)

41

LAWRENCE: <u>You whore, you slimy, filthy ass!</u>
(Looks down at his crotch. Childlike voice.)
I wet myself.

(Lights fade on LAWRENCE, rise on BARRY, talking to the audience, pacing, snapping his fingers each time he makes a point.)

BARRY: How did I get into OTC? Simple. Walked in, filled out an application for the OTC TV division. Bam! I'm a cable puller. Good cover. How did I get a place to stay? Simple. Talked to a camera man, Matthew Smith. Matthew put me up at his pad. How did I get a gun? Simple. Matthew makes a run every week to Virginia to buy guns for people for home or camper defense. Easy as buying pizza in Virginia. How will I shoot Wilkes? Simple. When Wilkes is live on TV, Matthew's camera is aimed right at'im. Thirty feet away, I'll be pulling cable.

(Lights dim on BARRY, rise on another area. BARRY walks into the light, pulling on a cable.)

BARRY: I'm tired of Wilkes' bullshit speeches.
(Sarcastic imitation.)
"Fellow OTC citizens, we cannot understand. We merely can experience."
(To audience.)
Look at that. Powerful Reverend Wilkes Martin is down on his knees. On television. Wait! ... Why's Matthew leaving his camera? He's not allowed to do that ... He's kneeling beside Wilkes. Talking about his wife and daughter ... killed by an 18-wheeler ... swearing to give up alcohol ... All three cameras are aimed at the two of'em ... Time to make my move.

(He eases behind the reverend and places his hand in his vest.)

Inside my vest, I feel my gun. My heart beating. My finger on the safety. Click it off.

(Looks around at TV audience.)

The audience is getting upset. What'd Wilkes say?

(He listens to Wilkes for a moment.)

He's gonna die? ... Ready for the Lord to take him home ... He's pointing straight into camera two.

(Wilkes' voice.)

"I'm askin' all you folks out there watchin', lay down your hate. I'm sick. My weak body is givin' out. I'm dyin'. Walk beside me. Win this sinnin' world back to truth."

(His own voice.)

Wilkes can't die. Not now.

(He starts crying.)

Yes, yes. I will, Wilkes. I can dig deeper into myself, give a little more. I can do that for you.

(He kneels and whispers.)

Only Through Christ! Only Through Christ!

(He walks back into his previous light, wipes away tears, and talks to audience.)

BARRY: Wilkes is dyin'. Says he'll be dead in just two months. All the money in the world won't save him. Mom sacrificed her retirement fund to build a new OTC gymnasium. Matthew Smith handed over his wife's insurance money for an OTC Theme Park water slide. Hundreds'a folks bought gravesites in Sue Lynn's Memorial OTC Pet Cemetery. But all that money doesn't matter now. He's dying.

(Pauses a moment to drink in the transformation.)

Ah. I feel him. Feel them both. Wilkes and Jesus flowing in my veins. I love you, Jesus. I love you, Wilkes ... Only Through Christ.

(BARRY walks into a dim light and examines his pistol.)

BARRY: Reverend Martin, sleep peacefully. The demons in that abyss cannot hide from me. Their unworthy shields will fall to he who chooses battle. I'll fight for you, Wilkes. "The Warrior!"

(Lights fade on BARRY, rise on JANET.)

JANET: Dear diary, the trial has begun. The jury is composed of decent Asheville citizens. The district attorney, Ms. Taylor Vance, is one of those splendidly intelligent Southern women, blending femininity of the old South with the killing initiative of a strong woman headed for a Federal Court position. All in one breath, she complimented my dress, asked how long Franklin owned his pistol, informed me they found a bullet in the pool house wall, and then admired my alligator belt. If you are uncertain whether you were comforted, devoured, or both, you are talking with a skilled Southern woman. Ms. Vance had the audacity to ask about me staying with my handsome security guard in our cozy cabin. Before I could answer she explained her name, Taylor, is actually a family name from a long lineage of lawyers, judges, and governors. "Y'all? We'll chat more later." ... Oh. Daddy's tie.
(She walks to her father.)
Daddy? Let me fix that grumpy old knot in your tie.
(She corrects the tie knot.)
There.
(To audience.)

Daddy said of all the names he submitted for qualified prosecutors, they selected the nosiest, most incompetent belle who can't recognize a retarded psychopath like Lawrence Greene even if you lead her by her tacky earrings. She may fool Daddy. Not me.

(Lights rise on LAWRENCE in court as JANET takes her seat. She watches the hearing, turning to explain to the audience.)

JANET: Ms. Taylor Vance primed the jury with a story. "Mr. Greene stole gin for his alcohol habit, stole their home security gun, cold bloodedly killed their dog, and in a desperately sick act, placed the decaying puppy on his sister's pillow." And of course, Ms. Vance supplied the motive. "Revenge! Revenge toward the very people who befriended him. Lawrence Greene feared he would lose his job over stealing to feed his alcohol habit. Mr. Greene had to stop Franklin Webster Kenny from exposing him. He stopped him all right. Stopped him by shooting at him, pushing him into the pool, crushing his head with the same shovel he used to both bury and dig up the Kennys' puppy. Bits of Franklin Kenny's scalp embedded in the metal."

(LAWRENCE plays with his fingers.)

LAWRENCE: Here's the church and here's the steeple, look at all'em people.
JANET: Ms. Vance boasted, "In fifty years of North Carolina history, not one mentally-ill person received treatment instead of prison, instead of death. Fifty years." Ending with, "Let's not break our record," and winked at the jury.

(Lights fade on courtroom, rise on BARRY, reading letter.)

BARRY: "Dear Wilkes, I hope when you read this letter, you won't be afraid of me. This week, I was inches from you with a gun in my jacket. I could have blown you away, but I didn't. I never will. I saw you at OTC with a beautiful Spanish woman. Death followed that same woman to Franklin Kenny. I fear she now brings death to OTC. If you can meet, leave your reply on the OTC Campground bulletin board. Address it to, 'The Warrior for Christ.'"

(Lights fade on BARRY, rise on courtroom.)

JANET: On Wednesday, Ms. Taylor Vance did what I thought no lawyer could. She spent an entire day making one point. "Of all the people at the Kenny residence, only Lawrence J. Greene's fingerprints were found on the shovel. Not Mr. Kenny's, not Lawrence's sister, but Lawrence J. Greene's." A full day for that one point. Once she finished, Lawrence's lawyer presented his counterpoint in ten seconds. "Is it not true most people using shovels, for whatever purpose—digging or murder, wear gloves? Don't leave finger prints? Thank you."

(Lights fade on court, rise on BARRY.)

BARRY: Wilkes failed to answer my letter. At first, that hurt me. Then I learned it wasn't his fault. The police hauled him away. On TV! Not OTC TV, but ... TV. The police pushing down on his head as they forced him into the back of their van. Handcuffed. Matthew explained newspaper reporters lied to the police that Wilkes was abusing people at OTC. Women, men, girls, boys. Lied Wilkes had sex with'em! Now, because of no good newspaper lies, God's messenger is locked up. Maybe there is no God anymore. God wouldn't let this happen. To a reverend? Uh uh. Well. Guess it's up to me to take matters into my own hands. "The Warrior for Truth."

(Lights fade on BARRY, rise on JANET.)

JANET: Etta took the stand. The prosecution confronted her that Lawrence's fingerprints were on the gin bottle, on Franklin's gun, on the shovel. Etta screamed in court, "All lies. They wuz paid off." They showed Etta a photograph of Horatio. Dead. Decomposing. "Is that your bed and pillow in the photograph?" "Yes ma'am." "And do you recognize that dog on your pillow?" "Yes ma'am, I do. That there's the twins' pup, Horatio."

(The light fades on JANET, and she walks into another light.)

JANET: I discontinued my antidepressant, so of course, my nightmares returned. Fragments. Like swimming in cold, chilled vapors. I can see, but there's no sound. A white porcelain vase trimmed with delicate blue violets. It smashes against a mahogany-edged chiffonnier.
(Looks to door as John enters.)
John? Come sit with me ... Yeah. Those photos upset me, too. I didn't realize Horatio met such a ... a violent—

(The phone rings, and JANET answers.)

JANET: Hi Daddy ... Talking with Jonathan ... Why are you at the cabin? ... A break in?—Are you okay? ... Who are you talking with? It sounds like Charles ... Uh, I can't think of a reason someone would search our cabin. We don't have valuables there ... No special hiding place for valuables ... Don't yell at me! If I knew I'd tell you.

(Reacts to John speaking to her.)
Oh. Just a minute ... John reminded me Franklin's roll-
top desk has a secret compartment.
(Talking as she receives information from John.)
Right side. Scroll emblem slides to the left ... Got it? ...
Empty? I feel violated. Here. Talk with John.
*(She hands phone to John and paces as John talks on
phone for a moment. John ends call.)*
What did Daddy say?

*(Lights fade on JANET as she walks to another light and
writes.)*

JANET: Dear diary. Our cabin at Gingerbread Acres was
vandalized. Papers, photographs, books, thrown on the
floor as if someone were desperately searching. I asked
John to talk with Daddy. The call upset him enormously.
He questions how Daddy knew his and James' school
pictures were in the secret compartment, since Daddy
had claimed all our belongings were already scattered on
the floor. I didn't follow, so John explained his logic.
Daddy and Charles were the people ransacking the cabin
... until we led them to the secret compartment. To the
receipts. "Southern Supply."
(She walks to the audience.)
There are pains that are peripheral in nature, that stab
at one's muscles. There are other pains that empty our
hearts, steal breath in an instant.

*(Lights fade on JANET, rise on court. Etta is on the stand
when JANET enters and takes her seat.)*

JANET: *(Whispers to audience.)* Etta is already on the stand.
(Etta's voice.)
"It was a white vase with little violet flowers. LJ give it
to me when I wuz fourteen and he was only sitz, 'cause I

stood outside Belk's Department Store one fall day, 'miring it through the window. He collected soda pop bottles to pay fer it. Nicest gift I ever got."

(Lights fade on court. JANET walks to a light and writes.)

JANET: Dear diary, not O'Henry or Faulkner could have drummed up such sentiment. Etta stared at the marble courtroom floor until even I imagined a dirt floor with thirteen little brothers and sisters begging for a morsel. Her vase of generosity. As soon as Etta had the mind's eye of her audience consumed by the injustices of North Carolina's poor, she juxtaposed her carver's knife upon my throat.
(She walks to the audience and imitates Etta.)
"Miss Kinny busted poor little Lawrence's soda-pop-bottle vase over Mr. Kinny's soft head. A million pieces. I swear to God. She killt that sweet man what wuz so good to me and Lawrence."
(Her own voice.)
The prosecutor pointed out no vase was found. But noted,
(Imitates Taylor asking questions and Etta answering.)
"Miss Greene? Thousands of tiny crystals were found in your carpet. Blood on the crystals, blood on your rug, on the shovel. All Mr. Kenny's blood. Can you explain what Mr. Franklin Kenny was doing in your apartment that night?"
"All them places, all rooms at the Kinny residence all belong to Mr. Kinny. He wuz checkin'em out, I reckon."
"Checking out your apartment?"
"Uh huh."
"Late at night?"
"I 'spect so."
"Was Mrs. Kenny also there?"

"Miss Kinny followed Mr. Kinny there and wuz all drunk and drug up and hollerin'."

"So, both Mr. and Mrs. Kenny were in your apartment?"

"Uh huh."

"Did Mrs. Kenny hit her husband in front of you, with your little soda pop vase?"

"She did, yes ma'am."

"She wasn't worried you were standing there watching?"

"Well, I didn't 'xactly watch her hit him. I stepped out to git Mr. Kinny somethin'."

"So, you did not see Mrs. Kenny hit Mr. Kenny?"

"Not 'xactly."

"And in the middle of all this arguing, what did you step out to get?"

"Huh?"

"You said you stepped out to get—"

"Somethin' Mr. Kinny wuz lookin' fer."

"What?"

"His pistol. Maybe."

"His pistol maybe?"

"I ... think so, yeah."

"You had Franklin Kenny's pistol?"

"I said, I wuz lookin' fer it!"

"For Mr. Kenny?"

"He asked 'bout it and I tode him I might could'a seen it."

"Saw it? Where?"

"By the garage house. Maybe in the dirt."

"Did you tell him you saw it by the garage house?"

"Mr. Kinny accused LJ'a takin' his pistol, and takin' his gin, and stealin' food from the house to live under their garage. He wuz accusin' LJ of everythin' that ever had went wrong jest 'cause him and Miss Kinny couldn't git along and I wudn't gonna be no part'a it! All I know is Miss Kinny and Mr. Kinny wuz fightin' inside my apartment and rich people buy off anybody they want and blame poor people."

"Miss Greene, did you yourself break your own vase over Mr. Kenny's head?"

"That's the most sick thin' anybody's said so far. No, Miss Taylor Vance. I did not hit Mr. Kinny. When I come back from lookin' fer Mr. Kinny's pistol, my vase wuz broke and the Kinnys wuz both gone. I locked my door and went to bed. And that's all I'm sayin'."

"So, your brother shot at Franklin Kenny, hit him with the vase, hit him with the shovel, and drowned him."

(Her own voice.)

Lawrence's lawyer objected. No further questions.

(Lights fade on courtroom, rise on Etta's apartment as JANET enters and talks to audience.)

JANET: Etta's apartment. The mahogany-edged chiffonnier.

(She kneels and rubs carpet.)

White crystals. Embedded in Etta's rug. Embedded in minds of the jury. The coroner said the vase and bullet did not kill Franklin. He was knocked unconscious with the shovel. But who would then push an unconscious man into a pool to drown? Someone covering for Etta? Covering for me?

(She paces, talking to the audience, similar to a lawyer addressing a jury.)

What is the difference between memory and imagination? If we can't distinguish, how do we live with that? Will my sons ever trust me? Do they believe I took their father from them? What if my eternal punishment is ... to never know what happened?

(Lights fade on JANET, rise on LAWRENCE.)

LAWRENCE: *(Strange voice.)* <u>What are all these stupid ass</u> <u>crayons fer you dick brains? Stick'em up yer ass holes.</u> <u>What am I supposed to do with'em? Eat'em? A red one.</u>
(He eats a crayon.)
<u>A green one. Now kiss me and I spit little pieces'a green</u> <u>and red down yer throats. I make you puke yer stomachs</u> <u>out yer noses before I's through with ya!</u>
(His own voice.)
No, no ... I can't let Larry back in me. Etta is the best sister in the world, 'cause she tells only truth. I never killt no one and rich people like the Kinnys are goin' to blame me as sure as Doc Clayton—
(Strange voice.)
<u>gonna do more fuckin' testes on me all cuz Mr. Charles</u> <u>push Mr. Kinny in the pool and hit'im with the shovel!</u>
(He hits his head with his fists. His own voice.)
Stay out Larry, stay outta my head. Please God, don't let me live like this no more.

(Lights fade on LAWRENCE, rise on BARRY, sitting and looking through binoculars.)

BARRY: So that's your big *Citizen Times* newspaper offices. Not so big, boys, girls. You thought you would get away with making up lies about good Christians. Tell lies to the police. Not on my watch. A decent man, Mr. Kenny donated food and medicine to Reverend Martin for his missions. He wouldn't have done that if Wilkes was evil like you lied he is. I do my research, too, fellas. Only I don't stop until I dig up full truth. Illuminate. You've been warned. "The Warrior for Truth."

(Lights fade on BARRY, rise on JANET.)

JANET: Dear diary, I dined with James and John at *Jour et Nuit* tonight. The head waiter, Émillen, asked if I heard

that one of their customers died in a plane accident. Émillen said the woman was from Colombia, visited their restaurant several times. I inquired—not divulging I was both lying and snooping—if the woman was Franklin's and my friend, whom we often entertained. He answered, "Why yes. Miss Andrade," adding he was sorry for our loss.
(Walks to audience.)
Was it drugs, pills, drinking? Or have I always lived in a protective fog? Numb to dangers enveloping my world. Dangers that Daddy's security, Nanny Nel, my own indulgences blocked me from grasping?

(Lights fade on JANET, rise on BARRY.)

BARRY: I wanted Franklin Kenny dead. I am glad he was facedown in his fancy pool, but I could not kill him. Grandmother Grotsky watches over my shoulder. I wanted Reverend Wilkes Martin dead, and he got locked away. I want the *Citizen Times* reporters to die—And they will. I wish ... It happens. There is a God. Sometimes he does what I wish. Other times, he orders me what to do. God? Do I take action against *Citizen Times*? Or will you? Send me your signal. "Your Disciple for Justice."

(Lights fade on BARRY, rise on JANET, writing.)

JANET: Dear diary, our time in the wilderness is coming to an end. We each found our strengths, our new beginnings. John rediscovered his father through fine novels. James found peace through friendship with Philip. Now that I am not drowning in pills and alcohol, I am rediscovering myself. I found a picture in Franklin's office desk. Us at our spot in the Yukon. I hear the young

Tlingit boy singing. My goose bumps signal I am still alive.

(Lights fade on JANET, rise on LAWRENCE, sitting in jail, stunned.)

LAWRENCE: Guilty? Guilty? ... No! No! This is <u>her</u> fault.
(Strange voice.)
<u>Whorin' bitch all dressed in uppity lawyer clothes with fancy talk. I torture her and Mr. Charles all through hell if they 'spect they kin get away with lies 'bout me.</u>
(His usual voice.)
Stop it LJ! Make Larry go away. Don't let him inside you.
(Strange voice.)
<u>All you filthy ass junkies gonna git it big time.</u>
(His usual voice, hitting his head with his hands.)
I mean it Larry, stay outta my head.

(Lights fade on LAWRENCE, rise on BARRY, reading from list.)

BARRY: One, buy a lighter. Two, buy gasoline to burn *Citizen Times*. Three, shoot and burn sinning reporters. Four, go on TV and tell women and men of the world they are safe. Five, visit my mother and let her be proud. Six, find Janet and see if she still wants to marry me. Only Through Christ.

(Lights fade on BARRY, rise on JANET, writing.)

JANET: Dear diary. Daddy is flying us to the coast. Swears he's finished with politics. When I asked if Franklin was in trouble with the government, he fell silent. I told Daddy I saw the receipts, the ones he took from the roll-top desk. "Southern Supply." He left the room to think. Returned and confessed, "Like your mother, you never miss a trick. In the end, I only fool myself. I made bad mistakes, mistakes we all paid dearly for."

It took time for me to gather courage to ask, "Daddy? Did I kill Franklin? Did you or Charles cover for me?"

(Walks to audience, alternates talking in her and her father's voices.)

"Why no, baby doll. How on earth would you get that silly notion? You don't have a violent streak in you."

"But I hit Franklin on the head with Etta's vase, didn't I?"

"You threw a few things. You know you have a bad aim."

"It's not comforting that you protect me so much. It's the people closest to me I don't know, who dash my dreams."

"The only way I know, baby doll."

"Daddy? You used to say ideas are more important than people."

"And when we die ... when our bones are dust ... ideas are what linger."

(She sits and writes.)

JANET: Dear diary, John shared his school essay with me. It is about the disservice parents inflict upon children, reading sanitized versions of fairy tales. Meanwhile, James went with Philip to the shooting range ... Guns.

(Lights fade on JANET, rise on LAWRENCE, talking to audience.)

LAWRENCE: Etta say, we gonna make appeals. Say no rich people's gonna blame me fer killin' nobody. But I can't keep Larry outta my head. I tode her over and over. There ain't no doctors in prison. She promised me she'd come back Saturday. Tode me jest hold onto my Bible and color them pictures she brung me.

(He puts his ear to the wall.)
On the other side'a this wall, spring flowers is comin' out.
Little puppies is most likely runnin' 'bout and lickin'
little kids and—
(Strange voice.)
<u>whores and pimps burnin'em with cigarettes and
laughin' til they piss on'em selfs.</u>
(His usual voice.)
Git a holt'a yourselves, LJ. Good. That's good, LJ. Calm.
Deep breaths. Calm.

*(Lights fade on LAWRENCE, rise on BARRY, carrying gas
canister.)*

BARRY: *(Anxious, out of breath.)* I can do this I can do this I
can do this. Number one, pour gasoline in entryway.
Number two, yell for reporters to step out. Number three,
light gasoline. Number four, shoot reporters if they
scream in too much pain. Number five, call Janet and tell
her I love her. Number six, tell women of the world they
are liberated. Grandmother Grotsky? Be proud of me.
(He retrieves lighter from his pocket and holds it out.)

(Lights fade on BARRY, rise on JANET.)

JANET: Yet, another Ashville citizen died violently. One of
the grocery boys at Mr. Lloyd's. Either accidentally or
intentionally set himself on fire ... I wonder if I met him.

*(Lights fade on JANET, rise on LAWRENCE, slowly pulling
off his belt and making a noose.)*

LAWRENCE: Keep real calm. Don't let Larry git inside you.
(He climbs on chair and stares up at ceiling.)
I smell them little flowers through that wall. Smells jest
like that mum Miss Kinny give me.

(He keeps eyes closed, puts noose around neck.)
It did smell like them little violets Mama give me, Etta.
You jest don't remember.
(He tightens noose.)

(Lights abruptly to black on LAWRENCE, rise on JANET, holding John's school paper.)

JANET: After Lawrence's death, his lawyer shared a file with Etta that the prosecution had suppressed. Horatio died from a perforated bowel. Ingested sharp bones of a small bird ... The twins returned to Exeter. Soon, I'll abandon this large, empty house. Downsize. Change venues. Move to the coast ... John's school essay. His translation of the French version of "Little Red Riding Hood." "Le Petit Chaperon Rouge."
(Reads paper.)
"The wolf killed the grandmother and poured her blood into a bottle and served her flesh on a platter. The little girl ate what was offered; and as she did, a little cat said, 'Slut! To eat the flesh and drink the blood of your grandmother!' 'Oh grandmother, what big teeth you have!' 'It's for eating you better, my dear.' And the wolf ate her."
(She steps close to audience.)
They were here all the time ... Wolves ... I wasn't looking ... See them? ... Inside ... In you ... In you ... In me.

(She moves to another light, sits and writes.)

September 7, 1987. It has been five months since Etta's brother hanged himself. I didn't talk about losing Franklin. Etta didn't talk about losing Lawrence. But then of course, Etta, with her intrusive, nosy disposition, wore me down. She inspired me to talk, and then naturally, she talked—incessantly. For the first time, I am hearing Etta. Actually, discovering her.

(She moves to another light, sits and writes.)

November 12, 1987. Dear diary, An inexplicable series of events. Etta and I both invited friends to join our soul-bearing talks. A peculiar assortment, as one might imagine. Tuesday and Thursday evening "baklava-and-cornbread talks." Seven women. Two men are considering joining. Maybe they will. Probably not.

(She moves to another light, sits and writes.)

Dear diary, I ran into Florence Robbins at a Biltmore House gala. I told her about our twice weekly meetings. I invited her. She declined. I surprised myself, spontaneously confessing that I detest the tiny peacock feather hat she wears in church. She laughed, hugged me, thanked me. Told me her husband, Edward, insists she wears it to please <u>his</u> mother, who gifted it to Florence from her vast ugly hat collection. Florence said, now that I had rendered a second, honest opinion, she felt braver, compelled to refuse Edward and his mother ... She joined our group.

(She moves to another light, sits and slowly writes.)

January 4, 1988. Dear diary, I chose not to move to the coast. Our addictive talks, gatherings are evolving, becoming daring. We examine evil that surrounds us. Resides in us. We no longer hide from what is vile. We embrace the necessity of abomination. Embrace our anger ... appreciate uncertainty, not knowing ... I feel stronger—I <u>am</u> stronger.

(She looks at audience for a moment, and then writes.)

<u>We</u> ... our group ... is stronger ... Janet.

FINALE

About the Author

A native of the South, DC Fidler has combined a career in academic psychiatry and cultural psychiatry with a lifetime of playwriting, acting, directing, composing music, and teaching creative writing and the dramatic arts.

He studied theatre, writing, chemistry, medicine, and psychiatry at the University of North Carolina at Chapel Hill, where he served on the faculty. He later served on the faculty at West Virginia University, teaching cultural psychiatry, clinical psychiatry, and acting.

A licensed psychiatrist, DC Fidler has lived and worked with the Alutiiq tribe in Akhiok, Alaska; the Al Moqbali Bedouin tribe near Sohar, Oman; the Kalkadoon Aboriginal Tribe in the outback of Queensland, Australia; and the Te Tau Ihu Maori Tribes on the South Island of New Zealand.

He began his acting career in outdoor dramas, summer stock theatre, and local films and television at age ten. He has written scripts and composed music for over fifty medical educational videos at UNC-CH and WVU. He has written twenty plays that have been produced in various community theatres and universities across North Carolina, Virginia, Ohio, and West Virginia, as well as St. Louis, Sacramento, San Diego, Los Angeles, Boston, Chicago, and New York City.

He consulted and appeared in educational productions for HBO, ABC, and PBS and performed in numerous stage plays including: *Hope is the Thing with Feathers, Night of January 16th, Thieves' Carnival, Blood Wedding, Our Town, A Life in the Theatre,* and *Fool for Love.*

Presently, he is a scriptwriter, film director, and medical consultant for educational films using professional actors to demonstrate mental health issues. In addition, he is an active member of the Dramatists Guild of America and the Charlotte Writers' Club.

Fidler previously chaired the Video Committee for the American Psychiatric Association and served as President of the Association for Academic Psychiatry. In 2003, he was inducted as a Fellow of the Royal College of Physicians of Ireland. He serves on the Arts and Humanities Committee for the Group for the Advancement of Psychiatry where he is co-producing a video series on the History of Psychiatry.

He is author of the textbook, *Psychiatry for Actors: Using Psychiatric Principles to Build Characters,* and author of the novel, *Boogieban.*

Plays by DC Fidler
- Voices in the Woods
- Guilt by Association (With RJ Casey)
- Three Diaries
- Master William Bowlinggreen and Company
- Shiraz
- The Anniversary of Miss Nanette Pringle
- School Children Hiding Under Desks
- Grams
- Camp Uni
- Boogieban (Two-Actor Version)
- Boogieban (Seven-Actor Version)
- Ahulaqs
- Elk and Wolf (With Travis Teffner)
- Santee Delta (With Travis Teffner)
- Celtic Crossing
- Stone Touchin'
- Daugherty Park Merry-Go-Round
- La Dynastie
- Gyges Solution
- Begat

Short Plays by DC Fidler
- Persons
- Cruise
- Mobile to Where
- Oman Truce
- Second Amendment
- The Greek God Club
- Four X
- Microscopic Misconceptions
- Drone Guns
- Moon Bugs (With Travis Teffner)

Novels and Textbooks by DC Fidler
- Boogieban
- Psychiatry for Actors: Building a Character Using Psychiatric Principles

Musicals by DC Fidler
- Pied Piper (With Lauren Horacek)
- Healer Man
- Medicine Show

www.ingramcontent.com/pod-product-compliance
Lightning Source LLC
Chambersburg PA
CBHW070747280626
47162CB00017B/2468